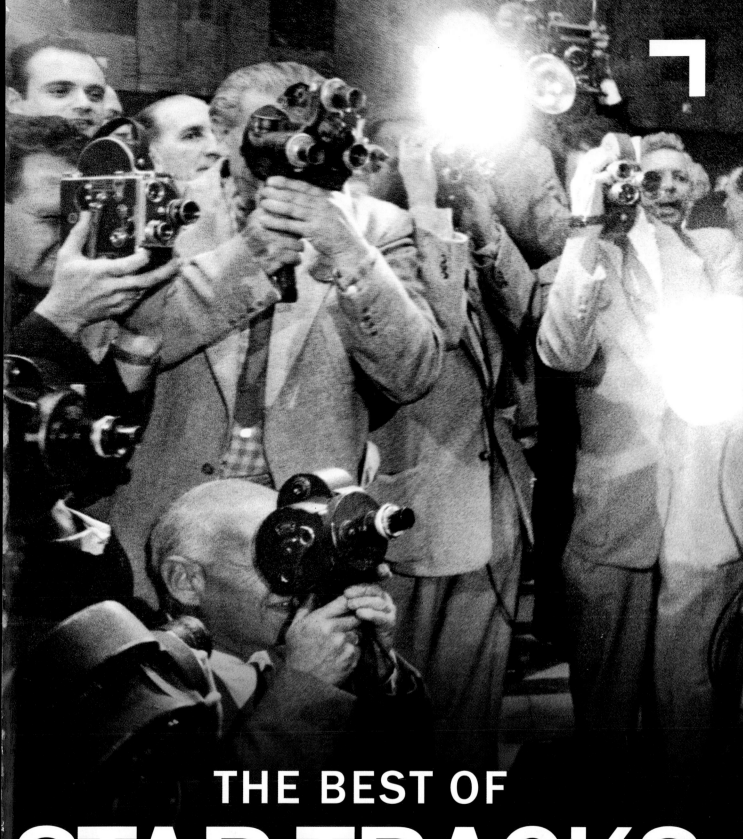

THE BEST OF
STAR TRACKS

THE GREATEST CANDID CELEBRITY PHOTOS

FOREWORD BY LIZ SMITH

Cold Mountain,
Hot Bash **DECEMBER 2003**
The camera caught *Cold Mountain*
costars **Nicole Kidman, Jude Law**
and **Renée Zellweger** letting
loose at a post-premiere fete.

CONTENTS

FOREWORD

BY LIZ SMITH

America's top gossip columnist takes a hard look at Hollywood and the paparazzi. Eventually, she likes what she sees

While the history of snapping stars in their finery at industry events, as well as on the sly in private moments, is as old as the movie business itself, there are changes to note. Once upon a time, for example, films reeked of glamor. Even gritty "realistic" movies looked fabulous. In darkened cinema palaces fans found their favorites at their peak. Photos of those stars in full regalia at a premiere, or carefully posed "at home" were fun, but they didn't represent the mythic image onscreen. A "candid" or unflattering photo back then might be a star . . . yawning.

Today it's all different. The star on the red carpet, robotically mouthing designers' names, going pale at the approach of Joan Rivers, defines the height of contemporary glamor—smoothed, buff, Botoxed, polished, taped up, pushed out, wedged in. Stars are not so beautiful now onscreen and must put the ultimate effort into these flashbulb rites; screamed at, booed if they don't cooperate, borrowed jewels trembling upon inflated bosoms.

Meanwhile the paparazzi taking their photos have become an even more contentious entity over the years. Back in 1962 one paparazzo in Rome punched Elizabeth Taylor in the stomach to "get an unusual expression" from the then scandal-mongered star. But that was not the norm. In the new millennium, "stalkerazzi" stop short of physical abuse, but what comes out of their mouths at the beautiful and the famous is staggering.

As for the truly candid snap . . . yawning has moved to nose picking. The romantic embrace is now two near-naked people on top of one another. But who am I to judge our changing times? I'm glad I'm still here to chronicle these events!

It was a nostalgic hoot to flip through this collection of paparazzi catches—the hairdos, the makeup, the changing partners. In some ways it's like the famous sequence in the 1960 version of *The Time Machine,* where the clothes on the mannequins change as the decades pass. But the mannequin itself is eternal. Each generation's gallery of celebrities is unique, but still they function to fill certain time-honored slots—the sex symbols (male and female), the "real" actors, the quirky flash-in-the-pans, the rare iconic figure whose personality and career is for the ages.

There's nothing new under the sun, not even the Hollywood sun, but while it shines, no light is brighter. When it fades, no chill is more profound. Or more public. But thanks to fans' never-ending (indeed exploding!) hunger to see stars grinning at their best, or casually being just like real people—with their lovers, babies, spouses—we'll always have a record of the way it was.

Here it is. Enjoy. And can you believe what they were wearing way back in 1985?

LIZ WITH . . . MARISA TOMEI, 2003

. . . DAVID GEST, LIZA MINNELLI, CHITA RIVERA AND ANTONIO BANDERAS, 2003

LIZ SMITH
ON THE JOB

. . . ANTHONY HOPKINS, 2003

. . . HILLARY RODHAM CLINTON, 2004

. . . ROSIE O'DONNELL AND TODD OLDHAM, 1994

. . . BARBARA WALTERS, 2001

. . . ANGELA BASSETT, 2002

Forever Jackie
NEW YORK, OCTOBER 1971
Photographer Ron Galella, who built his reputation (for better or worse) on his photos of **Jacqueline Kennedy Onassis,** called this windblown shot "the ultimate picture. This is beauty at its best."

CANDID, NOT CANNED

There may be only one sure way to spot a celebrity.

Look for the stretch Hummer? Nope; could just be a herd of teens on prom night. The Dolce & Gabbana dress? Might be *only* a socialite. The Prada-clad guy on the red carpet? Maybe— but it could just be a big night out for a manager-in-the-making currently ensconced in the DreamWorks mailroom.

No. If you want to ferret out who's really famous, watch for the telltale flashes and listen for the cicada-like whir of massed cameras: When it comes to pinpointing celebrities, it's the paparazzi who know for sure.

Click! It's Brad and Jen on a Mexican beach! Click! There's Madonna taking a dip in a mud bath! Click! Isn't that Ashton dancing in a club with Demi? Clickety-clickety-click-clickety: That, of course, would be Britney Spears, shopping, swimming, marrying, sneezing.

Hit That Line!
NEW YORK CITY, NOVEMBER 1974
Legendary paparazzo **Ron Galella** was ready for anything the famously short-tempered **Marlon Brando** could dish out backstage at a benefit for Native Americans in Manhattan's Waldorf-Astoria hotel.

Paparazzi have been at it for half a century, but they owe their name to lensmen like Tazio Secchiaroli, who strapped on a camera, hopped on a motor scooter and chased the likes of Brigitte Bardot and Ava Gardner around Rome in the 1950s. Italian director Federico Fellini immortalized the occupation with a character in his 1960 classic *La Dolce Vita* and called him Paparazzo (Italian for "buzzing insect").

They've been buzzing ever since. What's the draw for viewers? A couple of things. Paparazzi shots—even those at a premiere or a party—are more candid, less canned than tightly controlled glam photos taken in studios. At their best they capture, even if only for $^1/_{500}$ of a second, a spontaneous moment—a wink, a grimace, a look, a laugh. They can make the famous seem a little less removed, a little more real. "More people than ever want to see what the rich and famous do that is the same as what they do," says Randy Bauer of L.A.'s Bauer-Griffin photo agency. "They like to see them going to the gym, to Starbucks. That is why reality TV is so big right now. People want to see the way it is in real life."

Paparazzi is a growth industry. A decade ago there might have been 50 photographers on the hunt for notables. Today hundreds of shooters are focused on the famous. The bull market follows the enormous growth in media outlets—from magazines and newspaper-style sections to *Entertainment Tonight, Access Hollywood,* cable channels and the Internet.

Technology is a factor as well. The photographers who patrol Manhattan's SoHo or L.A.'s Rodeo Drive shoot digitally, which allows their agencies to stream thousands of frames over the Internet in moments. A picture of Gwyneth Paltrow and hubby Chris Martin cuddling newborn daughter Apple can appear on photo editors' screens almost before the new family has changed a diaper.

Only a decade ago a magazine might get 5,000 pictures of celebrities per week. Now it could be 50,000. "[Paparazzi] are becoming an industry of their own now," Kate Hudson recently said. "Even my parents [Goldie Hawn and Kurt Russell], were like, 'It was never like that . . .'" (As many celebrities can testify, it can also get out of hand: In Hudson's case several photographers allegedly dressed in medical scrubs and tried to sneak into her Los Angeles hospital room to get the first pictures of her infant son Ryder with rocker Chris Robinson.)

When paparazzi cross the line and become the more aggressive "stalkerazzi," some celebrities strike back. Recently Kid Rock allegedly mixed it up with photographers outside a Malibu club. Other stars just call their lawyers. Arnold Schwarzenegger successfully sued photographers for false imprisonment when they chased his car when he was taking his son to school in 1997. Jennifer Aniston settled a case in 2002 in which she contended that a photographer had climbed a neighbor's wall and took pictures while she sunbathed topless.

Still, the majority of paparazzi shots come from premieres, award ceremonies and parties—and though the relationship between photographers and the famous is seldom perfect, both sides usually get a little of what they want. Celebrity publicist Stan Rosenfield advises his clients, if caught off-guard, to play it cool: "Smile, give a good profile and try to walk away."

THE LOOKS

Some duos are flashes in the pan, others seem meant to last. However their passions play out, though, their trysts and tantrums—in public and private—never fail to fascinate

Red Carpet Royalty
CANNES, FRANCE, MAY 2004
Fabulous coifs! Astonishing physiques! Really, really good clothes! If there were a national king and queen of the prom, it would be **Brad Pitt** and **Jennifer Aniston.** The couple, says pal Melissa Etheridge, share "a joy of life."

OF LOVE

Lap Land
LOS ANGELES, SEPTEMBER 1986
Melrose Place star **Heather Locklear** clearly enjoyed taking a licking at the MTV Awards from her husband of five months, Mötley Crüe drummer **Tommy Lee.**

Do I Smell Smoke?
HOLLYWOOD, MARCH 2003
Why was **Ben Affleck** so distracted from fiancée **Jennifer Lopez,** shimmering in lime-sherbert Valentino and $250,000 worth of borrowed ice? Could be withdrawal. He'd recently given up smoking at the health-conscious J.Lo's insistence.

13

Rain Man
**NEW YORK CITY,
AUGUST 2001**
Always the gentleman,
Matthew Broderick
backpacked better half
Sarah Jessica Parker
across puddles
caused by a sudden
downpour to see
a play in Central Park.

Back in Baby's Arms
POMPANO BEACH, FLA., JULY 2000
Whitney Houston took a leap of love
to husband **Bobby Brown** after the soul
man spent 65 days in jail for parole
violations on a drunk-driving conviction.
Said he: "I'm going to spend the summer
with my kids and work on my life."

Daddy Cool **LOS ANGELES, MARCH 1975**
A smoothie at heart, **Jack Nicholson** (Oscar-bound with **Anjelica Huston**) told PEOPLE in 1985 of his longtime live-in love, "She's absolutely unpredictable and she's very beautiful. She's got this great natural sophistication."

Monster Mash **LOS ANGELES, FEBRUARY 2004**
Looking far better than she did in the *Monster* role for which she won Best Actress, South African **Charlize Theron** got a grip on both of her men—Oscar and her boyfriend, Irish actor **Stuart Townsend**.

Trancing the Night Away **LOS ANGELES, SEPTEMBER 2003**
In the merry moshing at the White Lotus club, **Demi Moore** and **Ashton Kutcher**
may have been moving to Aaliyah's *Age Ain't Nothing but a Number*.

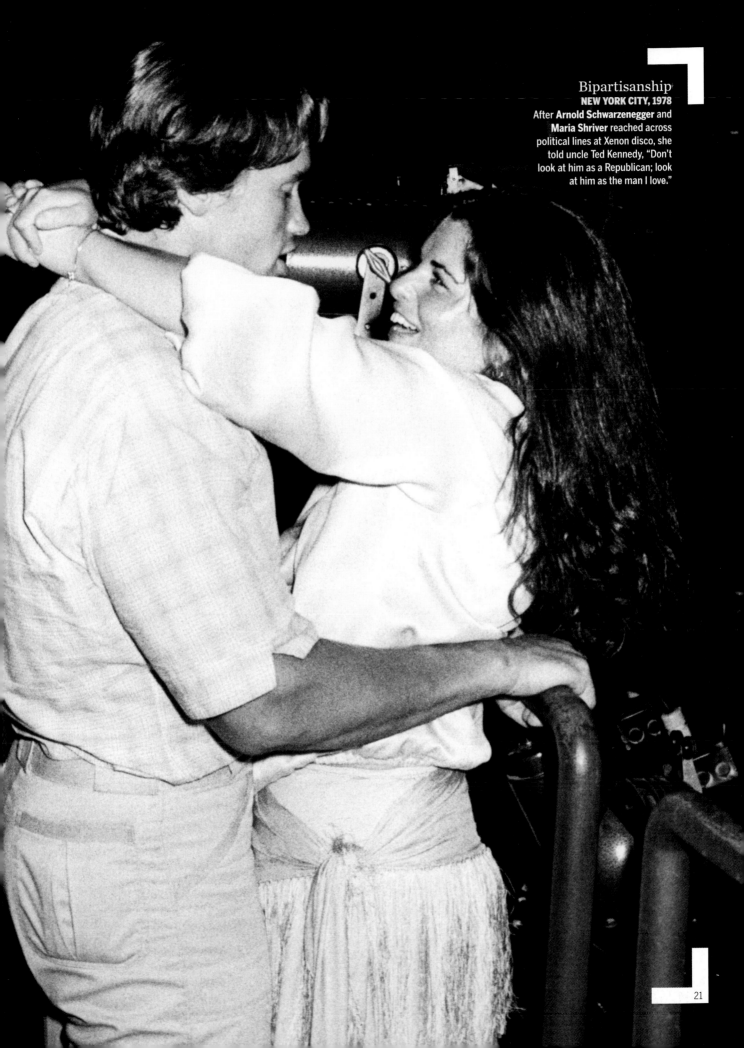

Bipartisanship
NEW YORK CITY, 1978
After **Arnold Schwarzenegger** and **Maria Shriver** reached across political lines at Xenon disco, she told uncle Ted Kennedy, "Don't look at him as a Republican; look at him as the man I love."

Shooting Stars BEVERLY HILLS, 1975
Melanie Griffith was 18 and **Don Johnson** was
26 when they made the scene after a Doobie
Brothers concert. They were, said paparazzo
Ron Galella, who took the photo, "beautiful
Hollywood wannabes who got to be."

Reading the Riot Act
LOS ANGELES, NOVEMBER 1987
Just a month after they attended this AIDS benefit,
Madonna and **Sean Penn** called off their marriage. "His
temperament is similar to mine," Madonna had said.
"That doesn't always make for ideal relationships."

23

DEMI MOORE AND ASHTON KUTCHER, MAY 2003

JULIA ROBERTS AND DANNY MODER, NOVEMBER 2001

LOVE, OUR FIRST SIGHT

When did the world find out that Brad and Jen were an item? Or Ashton and Demi, or any of these surprise couples? Here are the photos that tipped us off

WOODY ALLEN AND SOON YI PREVIN, NEW YORK CITY, FEBRUARY 1993

JENNIFER ANISTON AND BRAD PITT, 1998

BILL CLINTON AND MONICA LEWINSKY, WASHINGTON, D.C., NOVEMBER 1996

CALISTA FLOCKHART AND HARRISON FORD, LOS ANGELES, APRIL 2002

FRANK SINATRA AND MIA FARROW, 1965

MEG RYAN AND RUSSELL CROWE, SANTA MONICA, SEPTEMBER 2000

BEN AFFLECK AND JENNIFER LOPEZ, AUGUST 2002

ANNE HECHE AND ELLEN DEGENERES, LOS ANGELES, 1999

Waiting for the Train
NEW YORK CITY, JUNE 1993
Mariah Carey and music mogul
Tommy Mottola stepped onto rainy
Fifth Avenue, following their extravagant
wedding. They divorced in 1998.

THE MARRYING KIND

What? You weren't invited to
Mariah Carey's wedding?
Or to Matt LeBlanc's ceremony
on the cliff top? Not to worry—
the cameras were there for you

Southern Hospitality
**CUMBERLAND ISLAND, GA.,
SEPTEMBER 1996**
An intimate group of about 40 joined
John F. Kennedy Jr. and **Carolyn Bessette** for a top-secret ceremony on the
obscure island off the Georgia coast.

A Titanic Event

LAS VEGAS, JANUARY 2000 Five years after their extravagant Montreal wedding, **Celine Dion** and **René Angélil** renewed their vows in a similarly lavish Vegas ceremony. The Arabian Nights theme came equipped with camels and belly dancers.

Bridle Sweet
WILTSHIRE, ENGLAND, AUGUST 1992
Decked in head-to-toe Versace (the outfits were later to be auctioned for charity), **Sting** and **Trudie Styler** stopped horsing around and made their long-lasting courtship official in an 11th-century church.

Under His Thumb
SAINT-TROPEZ, MAY 1971
It was only rock and roll for **Mick Jagger,** but
Bianca Pérez Morena de Macias didn't like it when
he sprung a prenup on the four-months-pregnant
bride hours before the event, leaving her to
eventually retreat to the honeymoon suite alone.

Blanc Slate **KAUAI, HAWAII, MAY 2003 Matt LeBlanc** and longtime fiancée **Melissa McKnight** began their life as man and wife at a flower-laden site overlooking the Pacific. The couple, who spent the prior week relaxing on the island, were joined by Courteney Cox, Jennifer Aniston and Lisa Kudrow.

Suddenly Not Single **CATALINA ISLAND, CALIF., APRIL 2001**
Friends of **Brooke Shields** and fiancé **Chris Henchy** didn't know what to expect when their dinner in Marina del Rey turned into an impromptu boat ride. They quickly caught on when she changed into a Vera Wang wedding dress.

Whether they're strolling in the park or hitting the red carpet, celebrities are never too busy to pamper their kids

BABY,

I'M YOURS

Laugh In
HOLLYWOOD, FEBRUARY 2003
Goldie Hawn and daughter **Kate Hudson** got happy together at a party for *Dark Blue,* starring Kate's "Pa" Kurt Russell. Notes pal Rob Reiner of mother and daughter: "There's a gene pool that's definitely at work."

Roller Derby **BEVERLY HILLS, OCTOBER 2002**
Diane Keaton found no need to glam up for a stroll
around her Beverly Hills neighborhood with son **Duke**.
You can't be a style inspiration every day.

Bored of Governors **SACRAMENTO, NOVEMBER 2003**
A smooch between about-to-be California governator
Arnold Schwarzenegger and **Maria Shriver** left sons **Patrick** (left)
and **Christopher** out of the running.

Can You Hear
Me Now?
**NEW YORK CITY,
DECEMBER 2003**
Gwyneth Paltrow and
her baby-to-be got a
warm welcome from
future dad **Chris Martin**
outside a doctor's office.
Four days later the
couple eloped.

Squeeze Play
**LOS ANGELES,
SEPTEMBER 1993**
Kurt Cobain and **Courtney
Love** had a crush on daughter
Frances Bean. They were
photographed at the MTV Video
Music Awards, seven months
before Cobain's suicide.

Look Who's Walking
LOS ANGELES, NOVEMBER 2002
Bruce Willis was happily saddled with daughter **Scout** when the pair took in the prehistoric La Brea Tar Pits to see the remains of ancient mammoths.

Chug-a-Lug NEW YORK CITY, MAY 2001 Little **Oscar** is fascinated by how dad **Hugh Jackman** hits the bottle. The *X-Men* star's son visited him on the set of the romantic comedy *Kate & Leopold.*

Mudonna ITALY, JULY 2000 Eight months pregnant with son Rocco, her first child with English director-husband Guy Ritchie, **Madonna** took a rare two-week break and soaked away her cares mud-bathing in Italy.

Dipping in the Gene Pool CIRCA 1971
Michael Douglas was just a fledgling actor when the camera caught him here with his father, **Kirk.**

Soaking Up the Ray
ANAHEIM, CALIF., SEPTEMBER 2001
With his twin sons **Matthew** (left) and
Gregory, *Everybody Loves Raymond*'s
Ray Romano took the waters on
the Grizzly River Run ride at Disney's
California Adventure theme park.

HAVING A PARTY

Whether it's at a premiere, an awards show or an after-hours get-together, these celebrities know how to have a good time

Who Does Your Hair?
LOS ANGELES MARCH 2000
It was like Hottest Couples
night when **Jennifer Aniston** and
Julia Roberts celebrated the premiere
of *Erin Brockovich* with their dates,
Brad Pitt and **Benjamin Bratt.**

O Brother, Where Art Thou?
LOS ANGELES, JANUARY 2003
Kirsten Dunst and **Maggie Gyllenhaal** had a good old time at a Golden Globes party, and for good reason—they were both partying with Jake, Maggie's brother and Kirsten's date.

BEVERLY HILLS, JANUARY 2004
"It's awful to be the 'It Girl,'"
said *Lost in Translation's*
Scarlett Johansson (toasting at
a Golden Globes afterparty),
"because then you're the
once-was-an-It-Girl girl."

Frisky Business
LOS ANGELES, MARCH 2000
Elton John went far beyond the celebrity air-kiss
to greet a clearly enchanted **Elizabeth Hurley**
at the post-Oscar party to raise money for AIDS.

Better Daze **NEW YORK CITY, DECEMBER 1977**
In one of the great candid shots of all time, paparazza Robin Platzer freeze-
framed (from left) the designer **Halston**, **Bianca Jagger**, producer **Jack Haley Jr**.
with his wife, **Liza Minnelli**, and pop artist **Andy Warhol** celebrating
New Year's Eve at the notorious Studio 54 disco, the epicenter of the '70s scene.

Tease for Two
1989 One of the great mysteries of the era: What was up with **Madonna** and her flirtatious friendship with **Sandra Bernhard**? "Don't believe those stories," Madonna said. "Believe them," said Bernhard.

A Call to Arms
LOS ANGELES, JUNE 2003
Arriving at a premiere for *Charlie's Angels: Full Throttle*, **Ashley** and **Mary-Kate Olsen** were obviously on the same wavelength.

King of the World
PARIS, MARCH 1998
What's eating **Leonardo DiCaprio**?
A giant crowd of photographers at
a movie premiere. At the time,
months after the release of *Titanic*,
there was no bigger star than Leo
(trailed by actor **Gérard Depardieu**).

Party Like the Dickens **LOS ANGELES, JANUARY 1998**
With then-boyfriend **Ben Affleck**, **Gwyneth Paltrow** hoisted a glass at a premiere of her
Great Expectations. Staying literary, she'd later win an Oscar for *Shakespeare in Love*.

Close Shaves **LOS ANGELES, JUNE 2001**
At his 39th-birthday party at the Buffalo Club, **Tom Cruise** reached
new heights with his *Jerry Maguire* costar **Cuba Gooding Jr.**

Palm Pilot
LOS ANGELES, JULY 2003
If good things really do come in small packages, **Adrien Brody** must've had a fantastic time at the park with his new dog. The color-coordinating Oscar winner received the munchkin, a Chihuahua, from girlfriend Michelle Dupont.

WHAT'S

UP, DAWG?

Sure, they're used to getting recognition and applause from their fans, but sometimes even the most famous people need to get some creature comfort

I'm Pawed **PARK CITY, UTAH, JANUARY 2002**
Was this part of a bizarre dream sequence on the set of a
David Lynch project? No, just **Kyle MacLachlan** cozying up to
Popcorn, one of the locals at the Sundance Film Festival.

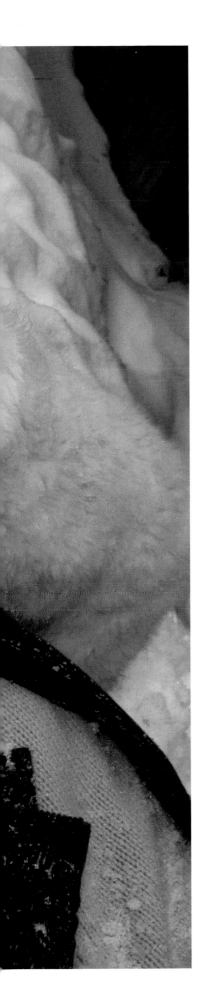

Saddle Star
MONGOLIA, MAY 2000
After running for the roses in the Oscar race with *Erin Brockovich*, **Julia Roberts** horsed around on the Asian steppes for a PBS show cunningly titled *Wild Horses of Mongolia with Julia Roberts*.

Together Again **WASHINGTON, D.C., 2001**
Former President Bill Clinton and ex-First Cat Socks reunited after a separation during the family's move to New York. The feline was adopted by Betty Currie, the President's former secretary.

Music Blubber **SAN DIEGO, AUGUST 1999**
Giving a new dimension to the celebrity air kiss, **Lauryn Hill** wasn't fishing for compliments when she dropped by SeaWorld with her children Zion and Selah to visit Shamu, the renowned killer whale.

Fetching Pair **SARDINIA, ITALY, JUNE 2003**
Heidi Klum and Shila, her Parson Russell terrier, enjoyed
a day out. They were visiting the homeland of Klum's
then boyfriend, Italian businessman Flavio Briatore.

Hitting the Bottle **LAS VEGAS, JANUARY 2002**
Penélope Cruz and **Tom Cruise** had a grrreat time feeding Atlas, a 5-month-old white
Siberian tiger from Siegfried and Roy's collection. Roy (right) would be critically injured in
October 2003 when another cat, Montecore, mauled him during a performance.

Heir & Hare
**GLOUCESTERSHIRE,
ENGLAND, MARCH 1990**
Prince William, 7,
cuddles with a furry friend
on the grounds of High-
grove, the family's country
home in Gloucestershire.
The estate remains Prince
Charles's official residence.

Kiss Piggy
BURBANK, CALIF., SEPTEMBER 2003
Hamlet, a 600-lb. pig, showed **Alyssa Milano** who's the boss during an appearance on *The Tonight Show with Jay Leno*. Realizing the dream of millions of teenage boys, Hamlet got to first base with Milano when the actress fed him a carrot with her lips.

Rock and a Wet Face

MAY 1974 Rock Hudson is remembered today as the first celebrity to die from AIDS. Eleven years earlier, however, the camera caught a happier moment with him and his Irish setter, Jill.

Croc with You SUN CITY, SOUTH AFRICA, 2001

A frequent visitor to the Kwena Gardens crocodile sanctuary during his stay in South Africa, **Michael Jackson** surprised staff members by agreeing to pet Rabatale, a 1,200-lb., 17-ft. Nile crocodile.

LOOK HOW THEY'VE GROWN UP

These celebrities took center stage in childhood and came of age while the world watched

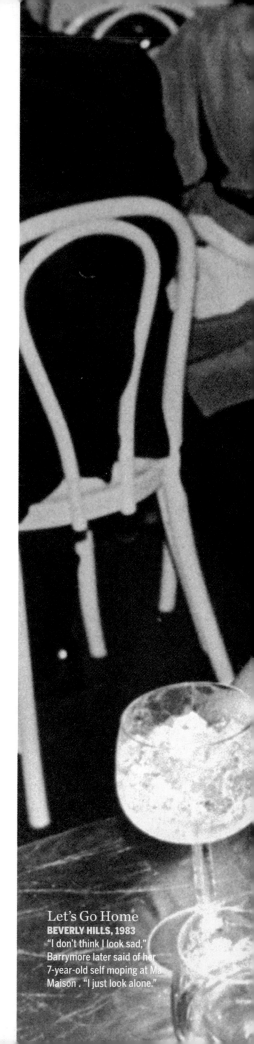

Let's Go Home
BEVERLY HILLS, 1983
"I don't think I look sad," Barrymore later said of her 7-year-old self moping at Ma Maison . "I just look alone."

DREW
BARRYMORE

From a dog-food ad as a baby
to *E.T.* to *50 First Dates*,
the fifth-generation trouper has
remained Drewly wonderful

An Alien Among Us 1981
The youngster clowned around with oddly disguised director **Steven Spielberg** while they were making *E.T.*

Legacy and Legend NEW YORK CITY, 1983
"I was trying to grasp everything about my family," said Barrymore (with her mother outside the theater named for her great-aunt Ethel).

Full Throttle
HOLLYWOOD, JUNE 2003
"I was having the best time with my girlfriends," Barrymore said of the two *Charlie's Angels* movies she made with costars **Lucy Liu** and **Cameron Diaz**.

Comic Relief **NEW YORK CITY, APRIL 2001**
"I thought we'd be together forever," said comic **Tom Green** (with Barrymore at a Knicks game). Their marriage—her second—ended after five months.

Different Strokes
**NEW YORK CITY,
AUGUST 2003**
"It's the most positive relationship I've ever been in," said Barrymore of her boyfriend of more than two years, **Fabrizio Moretti**, drummer for the rock band the Strokes.

Mother Love CAPRI, ITALY, 1971
"The world is pouring terrible adoration at the feet of my children.
How can I bring them up normally?" **Jackie** asked. Somehow she did.

Game, Set, Match FOREST HILLS, N.Y., 1977
"He had a rock-star quietness about him," a pal said of Kennedy (at a tennis match with his sister **Caroline**, far left, and his first public crush, **Meg Azzoni**.

JOHN F. KENNEDY JR.

For 38 short years, he was one of America's most photographed men—and as these pages show, he almost never took a bad one

Wedding March
BLOCK ISLAND, R.I.,
OCTOBER 1993
With girlfriend **Daryl Hannah** in hand, he hustled to cousin Ted Kennedy Jr.'s wedding to psychiatrist Kiki Gershman. After five years together, Kennedy and Hannah split up in 1994.

Breath Taker
**HYANNISPORT, MASS.,
AUGUST 1980**
His charisma could
produce unexpected
effects. Once, when
he asked a secretary
to help him make a
photocopy, she began
to hyperventilate.

Guiding Light NEW YORK CITY, FEBRUARY 1983
"My mother was very strict with me," Kennedy (walking with **Jackie** near Central Park) once told a waitress in Vero Beach, Fla. "Caroline could do just about anything, but if I stepped out of line, I got a swat."

A Squawk in the Park NEW YORK CITY, FEBRUARY 1996
Theirs was a volatile love affair. Months before they were married in a secret ceremony on a Georgia island, Kennedy and former Calvin Klein publicist **Carolyn Bessette** had a heated argument in Central Park.

Corresponding Love
WASHINGTON, D.C., MAY 1999
"I'm the happiest man alive," said Kennedy (with **Bessette**, at a White House dinner) of married life. Two months later both died when the plane he was piloting crashed.

Snappy Comeback **NEW YORK CITY, MARCH 1995**
Shields captured her own caricature at Sardi's, the venerable Manhattan
eatery. She was eligible to be included on the restaurant's
star-studded walls because she was making her Broadway musical debut,
playing against type as the trampy Rizzo in the revival of *Grease*.

Tropical Heat **JUNE 1980**

She was 15 when she made *The Blue Lagoon,* which created a scandal with its R-rated nudity. The controversy matched the uproar over *Pretty Baby* (1978), in which she played a child exposed to prostitution.

BROOKE SHIELDS

Once she'd modeled at the age of 11 months, nothing came between her and the world's cameras

Double Fault **JUNE 1994**

"Brooke is a wonderful human being," **Andre Agassi** (with Shields on the way to a Barbra Streisand concert) said of his wife. "I'm honored to be close to her." But the couple divorced after only two years of marriage.

Sweet Little Fourteen **LOS ANGELES, JUNE 1979**

Shields (swept off her feet at the Disco Music Awards by rock legend **Chuck Berry**) was famous for touting virginity. She even wrote a booklet for her Princeton classmates about staying pure until marriage.

Unidentified Fashion Object **NEW YORK CITY, FEBRUARY 1979**

According to the ads, nothing came between Brooke and her Calvin Klein jeans. But as she danced with a robot at Xenon disco, the slacks she decided to wear were, well, otherworldly.

Bathing Beauty
PUERTO RICO, SEPTEMBER 1986

In one year alone, the actress graced the covers of 30 magazines. "There are interesting looks," former *Vogue* editor Grace Mirabella said of Shields. "But these are great looks."

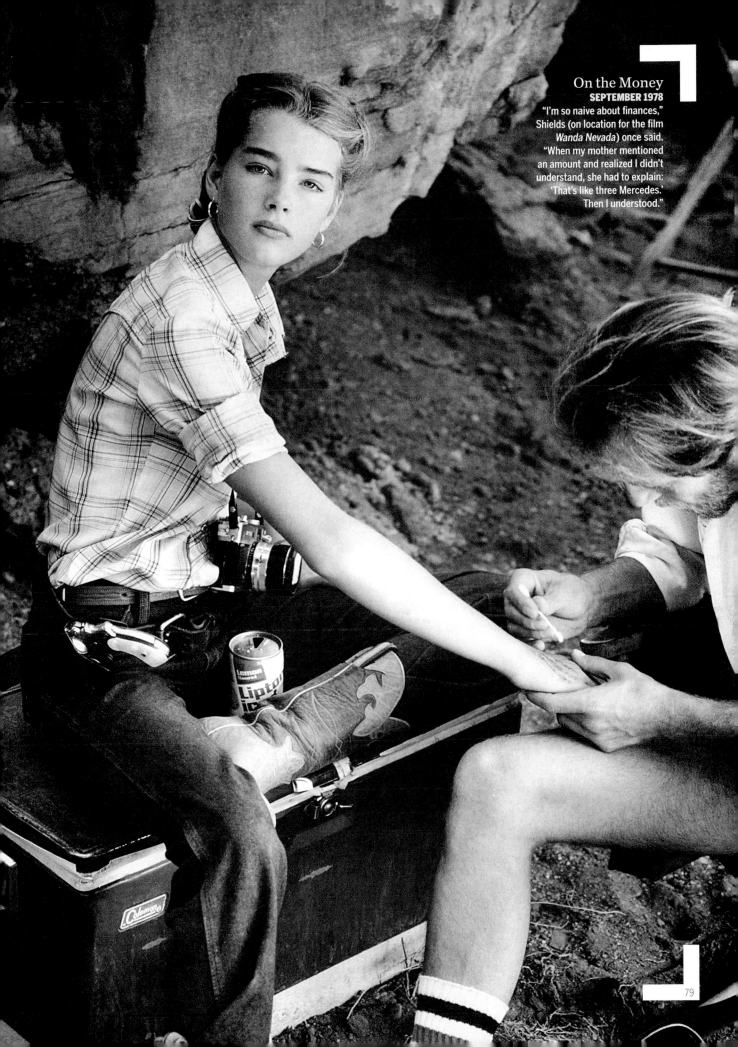

"I'm so naive about finances," Shields (on location for the film *Wanda Nevada*) once said. "When my mother mentioned an amount and realized I didn't understand, she had to explain: 'That's like three Mercedes.' Then I understood."

Return to Sender SANTA YNEZ VALLEY, CALIF., APRIL 1995
Lisa Marie Presley, with Jackson at a children's conference, said "Yes, yes, yes!" when asked if she was having sex with her husband. Still, she filed for divorce after 20 months of marriage.

Devil of a Time SANTA MARIA, CALIF., DECEMBER 2002
During a $21 million breach-of-contract case, an Edwardian-clad Jackson made like Satan for a photog. Earlier he asked for a break by telling the judge, "I have been holding it a long time. I really have to go."

MICHAEL JACKSON

From electrifying boy wonder to strange man-child, the controversial singer has changed as much as his face

Dangling Participant
BERLIN, NOVEMBER 2002
Jackson kicked off worldwide outrage when he dangled his 9-month-old son **Prince Michael II** from a hotel balcony. Later he asked, "Why would I put a scarf over the baby's face if I was trying to throw him off?"

The Three Masketeers **SANTA MONICA, APRIL 2003**
Jackson (shopping with son **Prince Michael** and daughter **Paris** at Sharper Image) thinks hiding their faces helps "to disguise them," says a friend.

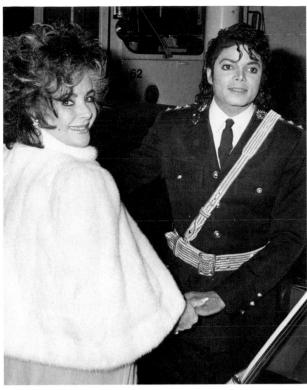

A Friend Indeed **LOS ANGELES, JANUARY 1986**
Pal **Elizabeth Taylor**, whose eighth wedding was held at the singer's Neverland Ranch, called Jackson "the least weird person I know."

Dangerous Liaison
LOS ANGELES, MARCH 1991
Though **Madonna** went with him to the Oscars that year and recorded a duet for his *Dangerous* album, she noted, "I would like to completely redo his whole image."

Time For A Break?
LONDON, AUGUST 1995
"We struggled along," **Diana** (with **Charles** and the boys at a V-J Day parade) told the BBC in 1995. "We had unique pressures put upon us, and we both tried our hardest to cover them up."

SUBJECTS

The fairy tale that was Diana's life ended in tragedy. But her legacy lives on in William and Harry—and in the moments that were caught by the camera

New to the Game
LONDON, NOVEMBER 1980
After it became known that Prince Charles intended to marry **Diana,** the paparazzi parked themselves on the kindergarten teacher's doorstep. She never became Queen of England, but she was the Princess of Op.

Royal Raspberry **LONDON, AUGUST 1988**
Determined to give her children real-world experience,
Diana insisted they attend regular schools and take part in
everyday activities like going to theme parks and playing
sports. "She wanted to show them another side of the
world," said a friend. At age 3, **Prince Harry**—mugging for
the cameras—seemed to have taken the lessons to heart.

Shy Guy WASHINGTON, D.C., NOVEMBER 1985
At a White House dinner, **Princess Diana** secretly wanted to cut a rug with **John Travolta**. The actor was "a bit shy," said **Nancy Reagan**, who whispered in his ear. "But as soon as they started, everybody stepped aside and watched in awe."

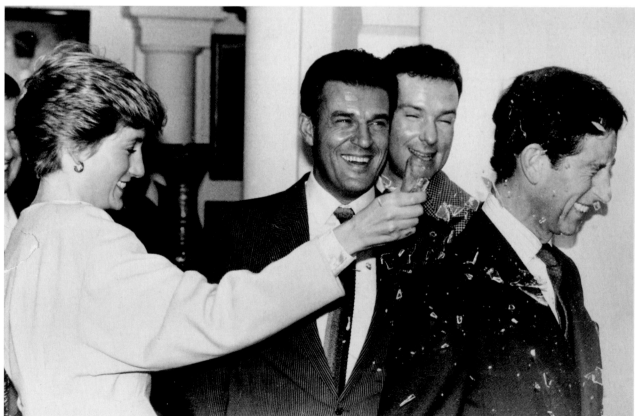

Shattered Class, **LONDON, DECEMBER 1986**
All was not as frisky as it seemed when **Diana** bopped **Charles** with a breakaway bottle on a movie set. She'd already confronted her husband's lover, **Camilla Parker-Bowles,** and told her she knew about their affair.

Great Expectations **LONDON, JULY 1981**
A gallant **Prince Charles** in his Royal Navy uniform shared a private wedding day moment with **Diana,**
ethereal in 40 yards of English silk, at Buckingham Palace. Said he: "We do this sort of thing rather well."

A Kick In The Grass
GLOUCESTERSHIRE, JUNE 2002
Prince William, then 20, showed a
princely penchant for multitasking
by chatting on his cell phone and
giving the boot to a soccer ball
in a friendly match with his pals.

Royal Pain
SYDNEY, SEPTEMBER 2003
"It's pretty feisty," said
19-year-old **Prince Harry**,
after being needled by an
Australian echidna. He was,
though, on his best behavior.
When two girls asked for a
kiss, he said, "I can't, really."

She Bangs
WEST HOLLYWOOD, FEBRUARY 2004
Depending on the setting, **Lara Flynn Boyle** can go from "rock and roll chic to '50s glamor," says her stylist Ken Paves. Boyle practiced her classic starlet pose as she arrived at the *Vanity Fair* post-Oscar party.

GLAMOR
GIRLS

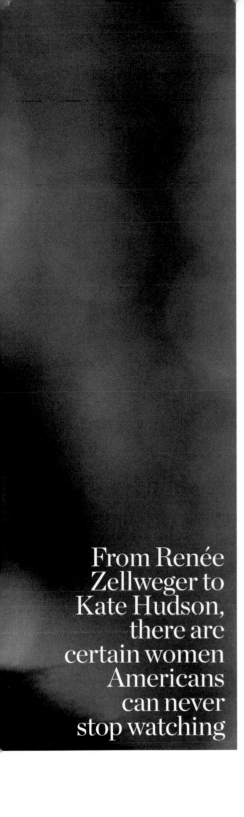

From Renée
Zellweger to
Kate Hudson,
there are
certain women
Americans
can never
stop watching

Literary Model **LONDON, JANUARY 2004**
Nightlife fixture **Kate Moss** dressed for the
decade as she celebrated her 30th birthday with
a 1920s theme party inspired by F. Scott
Fitzgerald's novel *The Beautiful and the Damned.*

Carpet Sweeper
LOS ANGELES, FEBRUARY 2004
Regal in Carolina Herrera,
Renée Zellweger swept past the
shooters on her way to winning
an Oscar for *Cold Mountain*.

Cruz Control
TOKYO, NOVEMBER 2003
Decked out in a gorgeous
Oscar de la Renta dress,
Penélope Cruz was on hand
for the Japanese premiere
of then-boyfriend Tom Cruise's
The Last Samurai, four
months before they broke up.

Hide and Peek
NEW YORK, OCTOBER 2003
Draped with a fox fur by Gucci,
Beyoncé Knowles was on hand
for a big-money night—the
unveiling of the $400,000
Mercedes-Benz SLR McLaren—
at the Trump World Tower.

Study Hall
NEW YORK, MAY 1978
Fashionistas watched **Jerry Hall's** every move as she slithered through a Stephen Burrows fashion show. The model is best known for her rocky marriage to Mick Jagger, which ended in 1999.

Tats Entertainment

LONDON, AUGUST 2003 Angelina Jolie showed off two of her signature tattoos at a premiere of *Lara Croft Tomb Raider: The Cradle of Life.*

Clip Job
**LOS ANGELES,
OCTOBER 2002
Salma Hayek**
topped her Narciso
Rodriguez gown
with a diamond hair
clip designed by
Fred Leighton for a
premiere of *Frida*.

Fur Trap
HOLLYWOOD, JANUARY 1973
Sonny Bono kept a tight grip on wife **Cher** during this appearance at the Golden Globes. He wouldn't cling for much longer—the feuding couple divorced in 1974, when she claimed he held her in "involuntary servitude."

The Palm of
Her Hand
CANNES, MAY 2004
That's where **Charlize
Theron** had photogra-
phers as she arrived at
the Cannes Film Festival.

JOB

Poultry costumes, women's wigs, sudden dunks in the drink—a star's workday can present its own special challenges

Simply Smashing **NEW YORK CITY, SEPTEMBER 2002** Life weighing you down? **Sandra Bullock** felt the same way during this trip to the Big Apple, where she did location filming for *Two Weeks Notice.*

Goodfeathers **NEW YORK CITY, OCTOBER 2001**
Do I look mah-velous in this costume? A little bit . . . little bit. *Analyze This* costars **Billy Crystal** and **Robert De Niro** hammed it up for this turkey day spot in Central Park promoting tourism in New York City after Sept. 11.

Keeping Her Guard Up

VANCOUVER, OCTOBER 2003
On the set of *Catwoman*, **Halle Berry**
showed stealthy reflexes during a
scene with costar **Benjamin Bratt**.
No stranger to comic book adaptations,
Berry will reprise her *X-Men* role,
Storm, in the upcoming *X-Men 3*.

Whale Rider

WANTAGH, N.Y., JULY 2001
The music wasn't the only thing flying through the air on the Long Island stop of **Moby**'s 15-city Area: One tour. The show included performances by various artists including OutKast, Nelly Furtado and Incubus.

Oh, Man
NEW YORK CITY, JUNE 2002
He's played a serial killer and a pornographer, so taking on the role of a transvestite wasn't that hard for **Woody Harrelson.** The actor got all dolled up on the set of *Anger Management* for his cameo as Galaxia, a cross-dressing prostitute.

Boy Troy **MALTA, MAY 2003**
Hi, do you guys sell wooden horses? In costume as Achilles on the set of the Greek epic *Troy* **Brad Pitt** took advantage of one of the many technological advances developed since 1100 B.C.

Buss Stop

NEW YORK, AUGUST 2003
You might date the beginning of the end of **Britney Spears**'s good-girl image to this encounter with **Madonna** at the MTV Video Music Awards. "It's crazy," Spears said of the public reaction, "but it's also kind of amusing."

You're the One That We Want
WESTCHESTER, N.Y., JANUARY 1976
When *Welcome Back Kotter*'s **John Travolta** appeared onstage in *Bus Stop*, teen playgoers were warned, "Don't talk or scream during the show. If any of this behavior occurs, we will stop the show."

The Big Plunge NEW YORK, JULY 2000
The drink was on *Sex and the City's* **Sarah Jessica Parker** and **Chris Noth** as the intermittent onscreen couple filmed a scene in Central Park. The February 2004 finale pulled a surprising tidbit out of the water: Big's first name was John.

The Few, The Proud
ARLINGTON, VA., OCTOBER 1994
Fulfilling a personal promise to run
a marathon at age 40, **Oprah Winfrey**
achieved her dream in the annual
Marine Corps Marathon. Winfrey
crossed the finish line in 4 hrs.,
29 min. and 15 sec.

TRAINING SPACES

Members of this group don't limit their action scenes to a studio lot. From Catherine Zeta-Jones on 18 to David Letterman on the diamond, these stars enjoy a taste of the sporting life

Leather Man **NEW YORK CITY, AUGUST 1987**
David Letterman demonstrated a stupid glove trick as his *Late Night* softball
squad rocked a team from *Rolling Stone*, 25-7. The talk show host would change
teams in 1993, leaving NBC to start the *Late Show* on CBS.

A Stone's Throw
LOS ANGELES, AUGUST 2003
Sharon Stone managed to keep
her uniform clean as she hurled the
ceremonial first pitch before a
Dodgers game against the Cincinnati
Reds. Luckily the team didn't need
her to slide into second.

000 Points **NEW YORK CITY, FEBRUARY 1997**
Accustomed to outwitting adversaries as Agent 007,
Pierce Brosnan got off on the wrong foot with this foe
in a *Late Show with David Letterman* bit. Brosnan
muffed a 20-yard kick, but looked great doing it.

Green Day ST. ANDREWS, SCOTLAND,
OCTOBER 1999 The hills were alive with the
sound of a victorious Catherine Zeta-Jones
following a satisfying round on the links in
the famous golf town.

Can You Dig It?
HONOLULU, OCTOBER 1985
Despite a Magnum-size effort,
Tom Selleck couldn't save his
team (his partner was top-
ranked player Hugh Foster)
from defeat during a volleyball
tournament at Waikiki Beach,
losing both matches.

Navel Maneuvers
BEVERLY HILLS, OCTOBER 2003
Matthew Perry gutted out a round of tennis in Merv Griffin's celebrity tournament. Perry might have picked up some pointers from friend Jennifer Capriati. He was one of the event's finalists.

Athletics Supporter
NEW YORK CITY, OCTOBER 2003
Britney Spears showed **Sean "P. Diddy" Combs** her team spirit as she wiped his forehead during a televised training session on MTV's *Total Request Live*. P. Diddy aimed to raise $1 million for children's charities in the next month's New York City Marathon.

ON THE WATERFRONT

Stepping out of the Armani and Versace into slightly smaller suits, some stars find the beach light as photo friendly as the bright lights

Angel on Board
HAWAII, SEPTEMBER 2003
No, **Justin Timberlake** wasn't drowning, but **Cameron Diaz** still swam out to his surfboard to administer some mouth-to-mouth. Says pal Sharon Osbourne: The pair "are perfect together."

Blown Out of the Water

MALIBU, OCTOBER 2002

One month before her 40th birthday, **Demi Moore** still looks better than most women half her age. The fabulously fit mother of three even impressed her costars on the set of *Charlie's Angels: Full Throttle*. "Oh my God, it's insane," says Drew Barrymore. "She has the most beautiful figure."

One Sweet Day
CAPRI, ITALY, JULY 2003
Mariah Carey took a break from entertaining her legions of fans with a sea cruise aboard a rented yacht. The vacation was well-deserved—the singer just wrapped the first leg of her world tour in Asia.

131

Aqua Man

MIAMI, JULY 2002

This was one dip in the Atlantic that *Titanic* star **Leonardo DiCaprio** (celebrating the July 4th weekend with pal Tobey Maguire) surely didn't mind taking.

Pitt of his Stomach **FRANCE, MAY 2004**
A chiseled **Brad Pitt** showed off his abs while taking a break
from filming his upcoming *Ocean's Twelve* with costar **Matt Damon**
(in water). The sequel is set to hit theaters in December 2004.

Blue Water **NECKER ISLAND, BRITISH V.I., APRIL 1989**
Another royal perk—free vacations. **Princess Diana** and 4-year old
Prince Harry enjoyed the surf on the private island. Usually costing
$7,500 a day, the stay for Di and her party of 16 was on the house.

Bond Bombshell
CADIZ, SPAIN, APRIL 2002
Weeks after winning her Best Actress Oscar for *Monster's Ball*, **Halle Berry** was in Spain adding the title of Bond Girl to her résumé in *Die Another Day*, where she played Jinx the CIA operative to Pierce Brosnan's Agent 007.

Skinny Dipping
**VENICE, CALIF.,
JULY 2003
Lara Flynn Boyle**
showed some
skin—and bones—
as she prepared to
spend a sunny day
at Venice Beach.

Alone in the Zone LAS VEGAS, APRIL 2003
Want to enjoy the desert sun without those other pesky hotel guests? **Britney Spears** just had the Palms Casino Resort close down a pool for her private use.

The Bottom Line CABO SAN LUCAS, MEXICO, MAY 2004

Forget about his & her towels. Honeymooning *Van Helsing* star **Kate Beckinsale** got so carried away by her marriage to director husband **Len Wiseman** that her bikini was monogrammed "Mrs. Wiseman." Prior to the honeymoon, Wiseman also gave Beckinsale's 5-year-old daughter Lily (with Welsh actor Michael Sheen) her own miniature wedding ring.

Love, Love **KAUAI, HAWAII, JANUARY 2000**

Andre Agassi and **Steffi Graf** practiced their sand game during a Hawaiian New Year's break. The vacation away from tennis served Agassi well: He won the 2000 Australian Open a few weeks later.

Splash! **MALIBU, AUGUST 1988**
Long before storming the beaches in *Saving Private Ryan*, **Tom Hanks** discovered a much more peaceful way to approach the sand. The actor frequently hit the waves near his Malibu home. In 1998 his production company began developing a screenplay about legendary surfer Mark Foo, who died riding a 20-ft. wave in 1994.

Caribbean Queen
BARBADOS, MAY 2004
With this serious strut onto
the beach, tennis player
Serena Williams was giving
off major movie-star vibe.
She may be on her way:
The volley girl has gotten
her feet wet with guest
spots on *My Wife and Kids*
and *Law & Order: SVU.*

CREDITS

Cover
Paul Smith/Retna **Inset:** Ron Galella

Title Page 1 Phil Stern/CPi

Contents 2-3 Alex Berliner/BEImages

Foreword 5 (clockwise from top left)
Gregory Pace/ Filmmagic; Matt Polk/
Wireimage; Dan Herrick/Zuma; Nancy
Kaszerman/Zuma; Patrick McMullan;
Arnaldo Magnani/Getty; Patrick McMullan

Introduction 6 Ron Galella
8-9 Paul Schmulbach/Galella

The Looks of Love
10-11 Mario Anzuoni/Splash News
12 Scott Downie/Celebrity Photo **13** Kevin
Winter/Getty **14** Henry Lamb/Photowire/
Starmax **15** Jon James/LFI **16** Kevork
Djansezian/AP **17** Max B. Miller/Foto
International/Getty **18-19** Ralph
Dominguez/Globe **20** Splash News **21** Ron
Galella **22** Ron Galella **23** Peter C. Borsari
24-25 (clockwise from top left) Ramey;
JFX Direct/Bauer-Griffin; Ramey; CA
Images/Fame; Bernie Abramson/MPTV;
Fame; Ralph Soluri/Wireimage; Dirck
Halstead/Getty; Paul Adao/NY News
Service; Fitzroy Barrett/Globe

The Marrying Kind
26 Jonathan Delano **27** Denis Reggie
28 Trustar/Reuters **29** Richard Young/
Rex **30-31** Patrick Lichfield/Camera
Press/ Retna **32** David Schumacher
33 Bauer-Griffin

Baby, I'm Yours
34-35 Bauer-Griffin (2) **36** Eric
Charbonneau/BEImages **37** Fame **38** Rich
Pedroncelli/AP **39** Val Malone/Wireimage
40 Paul Leander **41** JAG/Bauer-Griffin
42-43 (clockwise from top left) Alex
Oliveira/Startraks; MPTV; Furio/Lucky
Mat **44-45** Michael Jacobs/Disney

Having a Party
46-47 Alex Berliner/BEImages **48** Eric
Charbonneau/BEImages **49** Michael
Caulfield/Wireimage **50** Kevin Mazur/
Wireimage **51** Robin Platzer/Twin Images/
Time Life Pictures/Getty **52** Jeff
Slocomb/Corbis **53** Gilbert Flores/
Celebrity Photo **54-55** Mousse/MaxPPP/
Reflexnews **56** Alex Berliner/BEImages
57 Celebrity Vibe

What's Up, Dawg?
58-59 Flynet **60-61** (clockwise from left)
Jeff Vespa/Wireimage; Alan Sheldon/
Tigress Productions; Harry Hamburg/NY
Daily News **62** Sea World San Diego
63 Splash News **64** Jeff Klein/KPA/Zuma
65 Patrick Demarchelier/Camera Press/
Retna **66-67** (clockwise from left) Kevin
Winter/Getty; Charles Bush/Corbis
Sygma; Art Seitz

**Look How They've
Grown Up 68-69** Peter C. Borsari **70-
71** (clockwise from top left) Globe; Cour-
tesy Jaid Barrymore/Getty; Mark Mainz/
Getty; James Devaney/Wireimage;
Charles Wenzelberg; Kevin Winter/Getty
72-73 (clockwise from left) IPOL/Globe
(2); Brian Quigley **74-75** (clockwise from
left) Betty Burke Galella/Galella; Ronald
Lopez/Sipa; Coqueran Group; Tyler
Mallory/Getty **76-77** (clockwise from
bottom right) Nikki Vai/Celebrity Photo;
DMI/Time Life Pictures/Getty **78-79**
(clockwise from top left) Phil Roach/
Globe; Robin Platzer/Twin Images; Marv
Newton/MPTV; David Acevedo **80-81**
(clockwise from top left) Ramey; Kim
Maydole Lynch/MPTV; Ed Souza/AP
82-83 (clockwise from left) Splash News;
Bauer-Griffin; Kevin Winter/DMI/Time Life
Pictures/Getty; Peter C. Borsari

Royal Subjects
84-85 Ron Davies/All Action/Retna
86 Becky Sutton **87** NI Syndication **88-89**
(clockwise from top left) Tim Graham/
Corbis Sygma; Patrick Lichfield/Camera
Press/Retna; PA **90-91** (from left) Beirne/
Jones/ Dias/ Newspix; Rick Rycroft/AP

Glamor Girls 92-93 (from left) Chris
Weeks/AP; David Westing/Getty
94-95 Kevork Djansezian/AP **96** Yuriko
Nakao/ Reuters **97** Steve Granitz/
Wireimage **98** John Spellman/Retna **99**
Corbis Bettmann **100** Damien Day/
GlobelinkUK/Globe **101** Chris Polk/
Filmmagic **102** Kim Maydole Lynch/ MPTV
103 Vincent Kessler/Reuters

On the Job
104-105 (from left) Frank Ross; Steve
Sands/NY Newswire/Bauer-Griffin **106**
Andrew Stones/Splash News **107** Kevin
Mazur/ Wireimage **108** Bill Davila/Retna
109 Globe **110** Julie Jacobson/AP **111** Toby
Melville/Reuters **112-113** Ron Galella **114**
Lawrence Schwartzwald/Splash News **115**
Brenna/Jason Fraser

Training Spaces
116-117 Robert Trippett/Sipa **118** Geoffrey
Croft/Corbis Outline **119** Doug Benc/Getty
120 Lawrence Schwartzwald/Splash News
121 Rex **122-123** Tim Ryan **124** Kevin
Mazur/Wireimage **125** Jason Merritt/Film-
magic **126-127** Scott Gries/Getty

On the Waterfront
128-129 Flynet **130** Ramey **131**
Alpha/Globe **132** Big Pictures **133** Eliot
Press/Bauer-Griffin **134** Robin
Nunn/Nunn Syndication **135** Solar
Pix/Reflex **136** Flynet **137** JAG/Bauer-Grif-
fin (2) **138** Riquet/Bauer-Griffin **139**
Splash News **140** Tom F. Queally **141** Ron
C. Angle/Wireimage

Credits 143 Bauer-Griffin

End Page 144 Alex Berliner/BEImages

Back Cover (clockwise from top left)
Kevork Djansezian/AP; Reflexnews;
Ramey; Ron Galella

Editor Richard Sanders **Creative Director** Rina Migliaccio **Art Director** Peter B. Cury **Photo Editor** Lindsay Tyler **Editorial Manager** Andrew Abrahams
Designer Brian Anstey **Writers** J.D. Reed, Chris Strauss, Anne Marie Cruz **Asst. Photo Editors** Florence Nash, Nina Santacroce, Donna Tsufura
Reporters Danielle Anderson, Ivory J. Clinton, Jennifer Wren **Copy Editors** Will Becker, Kathleen Kelly, Joanann Scali **Production Artists** Michael Aponte,
Ivy Lee, Michelle Lockhart, Cynthia Miele, Daniel Neuburger **Image Specialists** Therese Hurter, Omar Martinez, Mark Polomski, Rob Roszkowski
Special Thanks to Jane Bealer, Robert Britton, Sal Covarubbias, Maura Foley, Margery Frohlinger, Julie Jordan, Charles Nelson, Susan Radlauer, Annette Rusin,
Jack Styczynski, Céline Wojtala, Patrick Yang

TIME INC. HOME ENTERTAINMENT President Rob Gursha **Vice President, New Product Development** Richard Fraiman **Executive Director, Marketing
Services** Carol Pittard **Director, Retail & Special Sales** Tom Mifsud **Director of Finance** Tricia Griffin **Assistant Marketing Director** Niki Whelan **Prepress
Manager** Emily Rabin **Associate Book Production Manager** Suzanne Janso **Associate Product Manager** Taylor Greene **SPECIAL THANKS** Bozena Bannett,
Alexandra Bliss, Bernadette Corbie, Robert Dente, Gina Di Meglio, Anne-Michelle Gallero, Peter Harper, Robert Marasco, Natalie McCrea, Jonathan Polsky,
Margarita Quiogue, Mary Jane Rigoroso, Steven Sandonato, Grace Sullivan

Poster Boy
LOS ANGELES, JUNE 2002
As **Justin Timberlake** discovered outside Hollywood's Latin Lounge, sometimes there's only one way to communicate with a photographer: sign language.

Back Story
LOS ANGELES, AUGUST 2001
The day before his divorce from Nicole Kidman was final, **Tom Cruise** faced the motor drives at the L.A. premiere of Kidman's thriller *The Others*, which he executive produced.